87x 9/21

Green Light Readers

For the new reader who's ready to GO!

Amazing adventures await every young child who is eager to read.

Green Light Readers encourage children to explore, to imagine, and to grow through books. Created for beginning readers at two levels of skill, these lively illustrated stories have been carefully developed to reinforce reading basics taught at school and to make reading a fun and rewarding experience for children and grown-ups to share outside the classroom.

The grades and ages within each skill level are general guidelines only, and books included in both levels may feature any or all of the bulleted characteristics. When choosing a book for a new reader, remember that every child progresses at his or her own pace—be patient and supportive as the magic of reading takes hold.

1   Buckle up!

Kindergarten–Grade 1: Developing reading skills, ages 5–7
- Short, simple stories • Fully illustrated • Familiar objects and situations
- Playful rhythms • Spoken language patterns of children
- Rhymes and repeated phrases • Strong link between text and art

❷   Start the engine!

Grades 1–2: Reading with help, ages 6–8
- Longer stories, including nonfiction • Short chapters
- Generously illustrated • Less-familiar situations
- More fully developed characters • Creative language, including dialogue
- More subtle link between text and art

Green Light Readers incorporate characteristics detailed in the Reading Recovery model used by educators to assess the readability of texts through the end of first grade. Guidelines for reading levels for these readers have been developed with assistance from Mary Lou Meerson. An educational consultant, Ms. Meerson has been a classroom teacher, a language arts coordinator, an elementary school principal, and a university professor.

Published in collaboration with Harcourt School Publishers

The purple Snerd

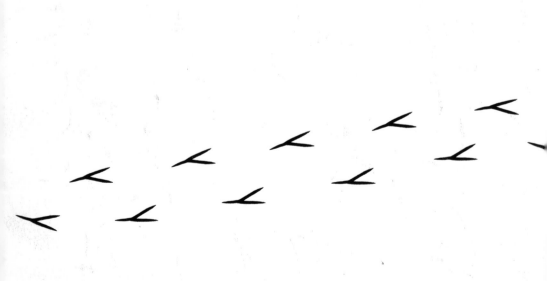

The Purple Snerd

Rozanne Lanczak Williams
Illustrated by Mary GrandPré

Green Light Readers
Harcourt, Inc.
San Diego   New York   London

www.harcourt.com

First Green Light Readers edition 2000
Green Light Readers is a registered trademark of Harcourt, Inc.

Library of Congress Cataloging-in-Publication Data
Williams, Rozanne Lanczak.
The purple snerd/Rozanne Lanczak Williams; illustrated by Mary GrandPré.
—1st Green Light Readers ed.
p. cm.
"Green Light Readers."
Summary: When an imaginary creature appears under the porch, Fern looks
in her book to determine its name, decides it's a purple snerd, and spends
the day playing with it.
[1. Imaginary playmates—Fiction. 2. Stories in rhyme.]
I. GrandPré, Mary, ill. II. Title.
PZ8.3.W67926Pu 2000
[E]—dc21 99-50810
ISBN 0-15-202654-1
ISBN 0-15-202661-4 (pb)

C E G H F D B
A C E G H F D B (pb)

One morning in March,
Fern was sitting outside.
Then all of a sudden . . .
"Snort! Chirp!" something cried.

It was under the porch.
Who or what could it be?
Some long purple fur
was all Fern could see.

It was smaller than her horse.
It was bigger than a bird.
Fern couldn't believe it—
could this be a Snerd?

The first thing Fern did
was to open her book.
Then she sat on a step
and had a good look.

Purple Snerds, the book said,
will purr, bark, and chirp.
When they eat all their sweet snacks,
they will snort and slurp.

Curled under Fern's porch,
the thing chirped, barked, and purred.
It snorted and slurped
like a Purple Snerd!

It said, "Hello, Fern!
I'm so glad we've met!
Can you find some sweet snacks—
as sweet as they get?"

"You *are* a Snerd!" cried Fern.
"Big and purple, I see!
I saw Snerds in my book
and now one's here with me!"

Fern and the Snerd
played around and had fun.
They even played Snerdball
outside in the sun.

Their time went by fast,
and the Snerd had to go.
"So long, Fern," he chirped.
"I'll come back, you know."

"So long," called Fern.
"It was such a fun day.
Bring more Purple Snerds
to my house to play!"

Meet the Author and the Illustrator

Rozanne Lanczak Williams always keeps a notebook with her. She writes down all her thoughts and ideas. When she needs an idea for a new story, she looks in her notebook. Rozanne hopes that after reading **The Purple Snerd**, you will want to write or tell your own stories.

Mary GrandPré kept thinking of her dog, Charlie, when she tried to draw the Purple Snerd. Charlie has a hairy face and loves to eat sweets. Somehow, the Purple Snerd turned out to look a lot like Charlie! Besides drawing, Mary likes to visit schools. She tells children about her work and shows them how to draw, too.

Look for these other Green Light Readers
in affordably priced paperbacks and hardcovers!

Level 1/Kindergarten–Grade 1

Big Brown Bear
David McPhail

Cloudy Day/Sunny Day
Donald Crews

Down on the Farm
Rita Lascaro

Just Clowning Around
Steven MacDonald
Illustrated by David McPhail

Lost!
Patti Trimble
Illustrated by Daniel Moreton

Popcorn
Alex Moran
Illustrated by Betsy Everitt

Rabbit and Turtle Go to School
Lucy Floyd
Illustrated by Christopher Denise

Rip's Secret Spot
Kristi T. Butler
Illustrated by Joe Cepeda

Six Silly Foxes
Alex Moran
Illustrated by Keith Baker

Sometimes
Keith Baker

The Tapping Tale
Judy Giglio
Illustrated by Joe Cepeda

What Day Is It?
Patti Trimble
Illustrated by Daniel Moreton

What I See
Holly Keller

Level 2/Grades 1–2

Animals on the Go
Jessica Brett
Illustrated by Richard Cowdrey

A Bed Full of Cats
Holly Keller

Catch Me If You Can!
Bernard Most

The Chick That Wouldn't Hatch
Claire Daniel
Illustrated by Lisa Campbell Ernst

Digger Pig and the Turnip
Caron Lee Cohen
Illustrated by Christopher Denise

The Fox and the Stork
Gerald McDermott

Get That Pest!
Erin Douglas
Illustrated by Wong Herbert Yee

I Wonder
Tana Hoban

Shoe Town
Janet Stevens and Susan Stevens Crummel
Illustrated by Janet Stevens

Tumbleweed Stew
Susan Stevens Crummel
Illustrated by Janet Stevens

The Very Boastful Kangaroo
Bernard Most

Why the Frog Has Big Eyes
Betsy Franco
Illustrated by Joung Un Kim

Green Light Readers is a registered trademark of Harcourt, Inc.

Green Light Readers
For the new reader who's ready to GO!